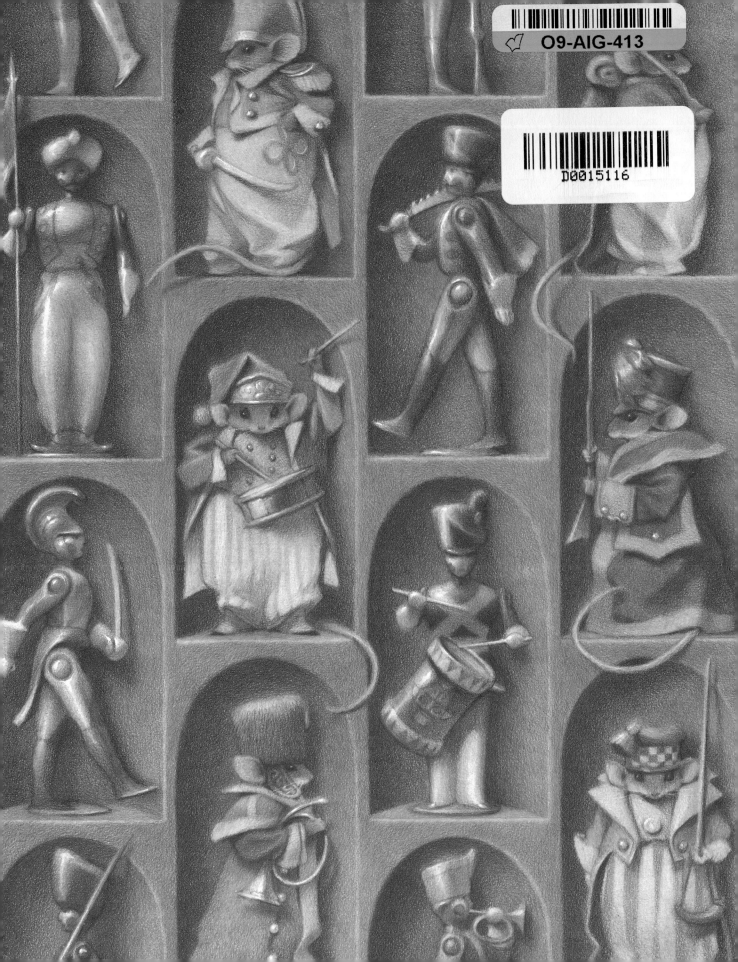

This book belongs to

The Duffy Family

Nutcracker

Nutcracker

by

E.T.A. HOFFMANN

Translated by Andrea Clark Madden

ILLUSTRATED BY CARTER GOODRICH

ARIEL BOOKS/ALFRED A. KNOPF   NEW YORK   1987

THIS IS A BORZOI BOOK
PUBLISHED BY ALFRED A. KNOPF, INC.

Library of Congress Cataloging-in-Publication Data

Hoffmann, E. T. A. (Ernest Theodor Amadeus), 1776–1822.
The nutcracker.

Translation of: Nussknacker und Mausekönig.
Summary: After hearing how her toy nutcracker got his ugly face, a little girl helps break the spell and
changes him into a handsome prince.
[1. Fairy tales]   I. Goodrich, Carter, ill.
II. Title.
Pz8.H675Nu 1987   [Fic]   87-45242
ISBN 0-394-55384-5

Manufactured in Singapore

FIRST EDITION

Composed by The TypeShop, New York, New York
Printed and bound by Tien Wah Press, Singapore
Art Direction by Armand Eisen and Thomas Durwood
Designed by Tasha Hall

The artwork is for Mom and Dad,
with love

Contents

Christmas Eve   3

The Christmas Presents   7

Marie's Pet and Protégé   12

Wonderful Events   16

The Battle   25

The Invalid   29

The Story of the Hard Nut   35

Uncle and Nephew   51

Victory   54

Toyland   61

The Capital of Toyland   65

Conclusion   72

Nutcracker

Christmas Eve

One Christmas Eve, Dr. Stahlbaum's children were told in no uncertain terms to stay out of both the main drawing room and the smaller one adjoining it. As the day came to an end and it began to grow dark, Fritz and Marie kept each other company in the back parlor and wondered what was happening. Fritz, who, like all older brothers, knew everything, pointed out to Marie, who was just seven, how odd it was that there were no Christmas candles around the house. And even odder, he whispered, were the muffled noises that had got him out of bed early that morning—rustling and rattling, and someone hammering—noises that had come and gone all day from inside the forbidden rooms. He went on in a low voice about how he had seen a little, dark-looking man steal into the house earlier with a large box tucked under his arm. Fritz tried to make the man sound mysterious and threatening, but Marie, used to her brother's tricks, knew it must be their godpapa. She looked into her brother's serious face and grinned.

"Aha!" she said, clapping her hands. "It's Godpapa Drosselmeier with a present!"

"Oh, Marie!" Fritz cried. Marie couldn't help but laugh.

"I wonder what he's brought us *this* time," she said.

Godpapa Drosselmeier was indeed a strange-looking man. He was short and thin, and at first sight his face was most unsettling: the skin was as wrinkled as a prune, and where his right eye should have been, there was only a big, black, plaster patch. Since he didn't have any hair, he wore a white wig made of glass—a real work of art—which Marie and Fritz might have thought quite beautiful if it hadn't been so strange. They knew, however, that when it came to clocks and watches, their godpapa was a genius. Not only could he make them himself, but he was an expert at repairing them. Their father was very proud of his collection of musical clocks, and when any one of them wasn't going quite right, Godpapa Drosselmeier would fly into the house, glass wig and all, and insert various sharp-pointed instruments inside the clock. This process made Marie quite uneasy; she could bear to watch for only a little while. But as soon as she would get up to leave, the clock would come to life, whirring and singing and striking the hour in a way that filled the whole household with joy. Of course, Marie and Fritz also looked forward to the small gifts their godfather brought them. They would run up to greet him, and from out of his pocket he'd pull a toy man who would bow and roll his eyes, or a box whose lid sprang open, releasing a little bird into the air—all sorts of wonderful things. But at Christmas, he outdid himself. Each year, their godpapa gave them a present more extraordinary than any before it. However, just because it *was* extraordinary—and very delicate—it would be theirs for only a day. After that, their parents would pack it up with great care and hide it away for safekeeping.

"I can't wait to see what it is," Marie said.

Fritz knew it just had to be a fortress with soldiers marching about the inner courtyard. He could picture enemy troops launching an attack with cannon fire and guns, while the soldiers in the fortress raced to their battle stations, everyone bravely at the ready.

"Oh, no," said Marie. "I think it's a swan with a gold collar about its neck that will swim up to me and eat cake and shortbread right from my hand."

"Swans don't eat cake and shortbread!" cried Fritz, in a rude tone of masculine superiority. "And we don't have a lake."

"It could swim with me when I have my bath," Marie suggested.

"I don't think so," Fritz replied. "We won't really get to play with it, whatever it is. Mama and Papa will put it away as soon as we've finished dinner."

Fritz and Marie both knew this was true. Still, they couldn't stop thinking about Godpapa's Drosselmeier's present. After all, Marie's only doll, Miss Gertrude, was so old and in such disrepair that she could no longer stand up by herself. Even when Marie leaned her against the wall or the leg of a chair, the poor thing would tumble to the floor as soon as Marie let go of her arm, leaving her in even worse shape than before. Fritz pointed out that at least she *had* a doll—he hadn't one decent fox in his whole animal collection! When he needed one, he had to appoint one of the other animals the fox—his lion or his bear—and it was so confusing that often the whole game was ruined. And his army had no cavalry—even Papa had noticed that!

Fritz stopped and looked out the window into the dark. Marie watched her brother grow quiet and serious and knew that he was remembering what night it was. He was thinking, as was she, of the many wonderful gifts Mama and Papa always had for them, and of how there was no need to fuss over what they wanted because the Christ Child took special care of everyone at Christmas. They sat perfectly still for a moment; then Fritz looked at his sister and announced:

"Well, I'd *still* like a fox and some horsemen!"

Turning around to see if anyone had heard him, Fritz felt an eeriness come over the room. He moved a little closer to Marie. Suddenly, the darkness around them stirred, and a soft breath of air touched their cheeks. The fluttering of large, gentle wings surrounded them; and though Fritz and Marie turned and looked about them several times, they could see nothing. Strains of the most beautiful music filtered into the room, but so faintly it must have come from very far away. Then, out of nowhere, a light brighter than any they'd ever seen flashed across the wall and vanished. Marie reached out and took her brother's arm. And Dr. Stahlbaum's children knew in their hearts that the Christ Child had been with them for a few minutes, just as He would visit all the children of the earth.

Kling-ling! Kling-ling! Someone in the hall was ringing a tiny bell. The doors of the parlor flew open, and light from the hallway poured in. "What is it?" cried Fritz. Marie squinted into the light, trying to see if the Christ Child had come back.

When their eyes had grown used to the brightness, the children saw their mother and father standing in front of them.

"Come now, darlings," they said, taking Fritz and Marie by the hand. "Come and see what the Christ Child has brought you."

The Christmas Presents

Dear reader—Fritz, Theodore, Elizabeth, or whoever you may be —I want you to close your eyes and remember how you got up on the morning of your last Christmas and ran to the room where all your presents were waiting under the tree. Remember how excited you were? How your heart pounded so that you thought it would burst? Well, that's just how Fritz and Marie felt as they walked into the drawing room and saw it decorated from top to bottom and filled with all the things they'd dreamed of. In fact, they were so thrilled that, at first, they couldn't utter a word! But that didn't last long. Soon Marie was shouting for joy and Fritz was jumping up and down, smiling from ear to ear.

Anyone could tell that these two children must have been very good all year to have earned such a lot of presents. The Christmas tree—which was twice as tall as Father—was covered with gold and silver apples. On every branch there were sugar almonds, chocolate-covered bonbons, and all sorts of other candies arranged in clusters to look like blossoms on the tree. And nestled in the hollows of the spreading branches sat hundreds of tiny candles that twinkled like stars, showing off the candy blossoms and fruit with a warm, flickering glow.

Marie wandered among the toys and found a most elegantly dressed doll with brown eyes and pink cheeks. She picked it up, hugged it close, and spun around, laying kisses on its soft hair, until she caught sight of another present. Hanging from one of the largest branches on the tree was a silk dress, exactly her size, with ribbons in her favorite colors all around the bottom of the skirt. Marie inspected every inch in the candlelight, touching first the sleeves and then the ribbons, until she cried, "It's *so* pretty! I can't wait to try it on!" But she'd barely gotten the dress down from the tree when Fritz, who'd already spotted his new fox tethered to a lower branch, could be heard giving the animal a stern lecture, so as not to have a troublemaker in his collection. He'd lined up his new cavalry to keep the fox from escaping. The poor animal didn't stand a chance against the rows of official-looking soldiers in their red uniforms trimmed with gold braid. A sword of sterling silver hung from every soldier's belt, and the horses they rode were so white that they, too, shone silver in the light of the tree.

It was a while before the children could sit still long enough to look through a few of the picture books that lay open among their other presents. Fritz insisted on turning the pages.

"Wait—you go too fast," said Marie. "Look—that flower looks real enough to pick!"

"Yes," said Fritz, "and that boy looks like he'd know a thing or two about commanding an army."

They were nearly at the end when the tinkling of a second bell sounded, and Fritz turned to his sister and said, "Marie, it's time!" They leapt up and ran to the wall at the other end of the room. There, on a large table draped with a curtain, was Godpapa Drosselmeier's present. Fritz walked around the curtain, but the present was hidden from every angle. Just when Fritz had given up altogether, the curtain started to rise very slowly. The children held their breath. And what do you think they saw?

At the center of a sprawling green lawn where roses, lilies, and violets grew, stood a stately castle with golden spires soaring toward the sky. Chimes were ringing inside one of the great turrets, and as if by magic all the castle doors and windows opened, one by one, of their own accord. Marie tapped Fritz's arm and pointed to a room where miniature lords and ladies moved about, wearing long velvet robes, tiny crowns, and feathered hats. In the great hall at the center of the castle, children were dancing to the chimes, while in the window of one of the very top floors, a man in an emerald-green cape popped up and waved to them. And after him, most astonishing of all, a tiny version of Godpapa Drosselmeier himself appeared in the castle entrance and then vanished back inside.

The thumb-sized people in the castle looked like they were having such a wonderful time that Fritz said, "Godpapa Drosselmeier, I want to go inside the castle too." But the old man laughed and told Fritz that not even his godson's foot could fit inside the front door, let alone the rest of him.

After they had all watched the children do their dance, the man wave from the high window, and Godpapa Drosselmeier come to the door over and over again, Fritz grew impatient. "Godpapa," he said, "now make the doll who looks like you come out of the side door instead."

"I'm sorry, Fritz. It can't be done," Godpapa Drosselmeier replied.

"In that case," said Fritz, "have the man in green dance with the others."

Drosselmeier scratched his ear. "I'm afraid that's impossible," he said.

Fritz looked down at the floor, thinking. "Godpapa," he said after a moment, "since I'm too big to go in, make the children come out into the garden so I can get a better look at them."

"No," cried his godpapa, "you don't understand! My mechanical people can do only one thing and that's all!"

"Is that so?" said Fritz. "Well! You can have your castle and everything in it! *My* soldiers can go where I like and do as I please. They're not prisoners in a house."

10

Fritz turned on his heel and went to play with his cavalry. Marie had left too. A short while before, she had slipped away to her other presents; but, unlike Fritz, she had not wanted anyone to notice.

Drosselmeier was annoyed and hurt that his favorite godchildren didn't appreciate all the care he had put into their gift. "Well!" he said in a huff, "such a creation is obviously wasted on children. I might as well put it away." But Mother, who understood how easily bored children are, asked him to show her how everything worked. By the time Drosselmeier had taken each piece apart, explained it, and reassembled it, he'd forgotten all about being angry. He went over to where Fritz and Marie were playing and gave each of them delightful, golden-brown men and women whose arms, legs, and hands were made of delicious-smelling ginger cake and who smiled up at the children with mouths of vanilla frosting.

Marie's Pet and Protégé

If truth be told, boredom wasn't the only reason Marie had crept away from the castle. Curiosity, too, had drawn her back to the tree. Now that Fritz's soldiers were marching in another part of the room, Marie could turn her attention to a toy that had been patiently waiting its turn to be noticed. Her heart immediately went out to the little man who was all by himself and almost totally hidden by the other presents. His body was much too big for his slender legs, and his head was all out of proportion with the rest of him; but for Marie, it was love at first sight. She could tell by his clothes that he was someone who loved beautiful things. He had on a soldier's uniform, but it was different from all the others: scarlet with gold trim and pants to match, and on his feet he wore boots that fit so well, they could have been painted on. The short coat that fell from his shoulders looked wooden and stiff and clashed with the smart uniform, as did his cap. And his tall cap of bright gold seemed quite imposing for a soldier. But Marie didn't mind. After all, there were times when Godpapa Drosselmeier rushed into the house in a terribly old, black cloak and a dreadfully solemn cap, and it didn't make him any less of a good godpapa. She could tell the little man had a fine character by the kind expression in his prominent blue eyes, and the smile that

12

beamed steadily from his red lips framed by his long white beard.

"Papa?" Marie asked, holding up her new treasure. "Who is this sitting under the tree?"

Papa knelt down next to Marie and said, "That fellow is going to crack nuts for us. He's a present for you children." He took the little man and held him by the cloak so that his mouth opened very wide. Then he told Marie to place a nut between his two rows of white teeth. Seconds later, there was a quick crack, and the shells fell to the floor, leaving only the tender meat.

"He is following in his father's footsteps," Dr. Stahlbaum said. "He's from the Nutcracker family." Marie ate the nutmeat greedily and patted the bearded cheek in thanks. "Since you're so fond of him, Marie," Father said, "you may be the one to take care of him—as long as you share him with Louise and Fritz."

Delighted, Marie gave the little man a hug and had him crack some more nuts, making sure she picked out the smallest so he wouldn't hurt himself. Then her older sister, Louise, came over to see what Marie was doing, and the little man continued to smile politely and cracked nuts for Louise as well.

By this time, Fritz was worn out from drilling his soldiers and asked his sisters if he could try the new toy. The little man was passed among the three of them, and Fritz laughed at how funny the Nutcracker looked with his mouth open wide, a nut sitting in the middle of it. So whenever his turn came, he searched the bowl for the biggest and hardest nuts he could find. On one of Fritz's turns, there was a different cracking sound, and three teeth fell out of the Nutcracker's mouth.

"Oh, no!" cried Marie. She took the Nutcracker away from her brother and sighed when she saw his jaw was now loose and wobbly. "The poor thing," she said, and was so sorry for him she began to cry.

"What good is he?" cried Fritz. "He calls himself a nutcracker and doesn't even last *one day*! Hand him over, Marie. I'll make him crack nuts. I don't care if all his teeth fall out and his jaw drops off!"

"No!" shouted Marie through her tears. "Leave him alone. You're horrible. You've already had one of your soldiers shot— and," she added, "you beat your horses!"

"All in the line of duty," said Fritz. "Girls don't know about things like that. Hand him over, Marie. He belongs to me too!"

Marie turned away from Fritz and gently wrapped the Nutcracker up in a lace handkerchief Mama had pinned to her dress.

"Marie!" Fritz shouted impatiently.

"What seems to be the problem?" asked Father, standing over them, a stern look on his face. Mother came over quickly too, her eyebrows raised, and Drosselmeier followed, wanting to know the cause of such commotion. Fritz and Marie in turn told their versions of what happened.

Father stroked his chin, considering the situation. After a moment, he said, "Fritz is right, Marie. The Nutcracker is as much his as it is yours." Then he turned to Fritz. "I've entrusted the care of the Nut-cracker to Marie," he said. "So you'll have to listen to her if she thinks he's had enough. Besides," he continued, "a good soldier knows better than to send a wounded man into battle. I'm surprised at you."

Fritz was ashamed and left to make sure his sol-diers were camped in a safe place for the night. Marie picked up the Nutcracker's lost teeth and secured his wobbly chin with a white rib-bon from her dress. Then she wrapped him up in her handkerchief even more ten-derly than before, rocked him in

her arms, and showed him one of the picture books to take his mind off his injuries.

"How can you make such a fuss over that ugly little man?"

Marie looked up and saw Godpapa Drosselmeier standing over her. He was laughing loudly and pointing his finger at the bandaged figure in Marie's lap. Marie felt her cheeks grow hot. She looked up at her godpapa and thought of what an ugly expression he had while making fun of her small friend—not at all like the patient, kind smile of the Nutcracker. "Who knows, Godpapa?" she said. "Maybe if you had beautiful clothes like the Nutcracker, you'd be almost as handsome as he is."

Hearing this, Mother and Father laughed so hard they held their sides. But Godpapa Drosselmeier did not think it was in the least funny. He was no longer laughing, and his nose had gone bright red.

Wonderful Events

We should mention that in the drawing room stood a tall cabinet with doors made of glass, and it was in this cabinet that all the children's Christmas presents were put each year for safekeeping. Though Louise had been a very little girl when Papa had it built, she could still remember watching the workmen place the long sheets of clear glass in each door. When they'd finished, the cabinet looked so splendid that Louise had thought her presents looked even more beautiful on the polished wooden shelves, behind the glass, then they did in her hand. The highest shelves, beyond the reach of small children, were reserved for Godpapa Drosselmeier's presents. Right below them sat the picture books. The two lower shelves were just the right height for Fritz and Marie, so Fritz set up barracks for his troops on the higher one, letting Marie have the bottom one for her dolls.

I don't know if you have a special room for your dolls, dear reader, but Marie had really thought of everything. In a corner of her shelf, there was a flowered sofa, a number of dainty, hand-carved chairs, a silver tea-cart, and a lovely white canopy bed. Tiny pictures decorated the walls of the room, and both Marie's new doll, Miss Clara, and the veteran Miss Gertrude seemed delighted with their fine accommodations.

By the time the children were coaxed away from their toys, it was almost midnight, and Godpapa Drosselmeier was nowhere to be found. Fritz and Marie were lingering by the glass cupboard when Mama reminded them it was long past their bedtime.

"Coming, Mama," called Fritz, taking a last look at his new soldiers. "My men are dog tired and need their sleep," he said to Marie. "But they'll stay at attention as long as I'm here." Duly impressed by the stamina of his men, Fritz turned and went upstairs to bed. But Marie begged her mother for a few more minutes to get all her toys properly settled on the first floor of the cabinet. Marie was a good and sensible child, so her mother allowed her to stay up a little longer. She kissed her daughter good night and put out all the lights and candles but one, overhead, so Marie would have a soft light by which to play.

"Don't be too long, Marie, or you'll be tired in the morning," her mother called as she started up the stairs. As soon as her mother was out of sight, Marie unwrapped the Nutcracker, who had been resting in her handkerchief, and examined his wounds. He was very pale, but he still had a kind, melancholy smile that pierced Marie's heart.

"Oh, Nutcracker," she whispered, "please don't be angry with Fritz. He didn't mean to hurt you. It's just that all his soldiering has left its mark. Underneath, he's really a very nice boy. Don't worry. I'll take care of you. We'll get your teeth fixed and your shoulder set right. Godpapa Drosselmeier will see to that and—"

Marie stopped short and blinked. She could have sworn that at the mention of Godpapa Drosselmeier, the Nutcracker had made a horrible face. His blue eyes had flashed, and his mouth and nose had twisted with revulsion. It had been only for an instant, and just as Marie started to feel afraid, she saw that her dear Nutcracker had the same kind expression he always had. Marie looked up at the ceiling lamp and decided there had been a draft that made the light flicker and her eyes play tricks on her.

"How silly of me!" she said, glancing around the room and then back at the Nutcracker. "Wooden dolls can't make faces. Why should I be frightened of my dear friend?" She adjusted his bandage and went over to the shelf where her dolls were. "As I was saying—in order to get better, you have to rest." Then she looked at her new doll, who was all ready to be placed in her big, comfortable bed, and said, "Won't you do me a favor, Miss Clara, and give your bed to poor, sick Nutcracker? A lady with cheeks as rosy and plump as yours should have no problem sleeping on the sofa."

Miss Clara, however, looked quite superior and made no response. "Well," Marie said, "I was only being polite." And with that, she took the bed, moved it closer, and laid the Nutcracker tenderly down on the lace pillow. Taking another ribbon from her dress, she wrapped it around his damaged shoulder and pulled the covers up to tuck him in. Miss Clara looked more disdainful than ever, so Marie picked up the bed.

"We can't have that nasty Clara scowling at you," she said, and moved him to the upper shelf near the village where Fritz had his army barracks. With the Nutcracker settled down for the night, Marie closed the cabinet and turned to go to bed. She hadn't taken two steps when— reader, do listen carefully—a low rustling and rattling and the sound of whispering came from behind the drapes, under the chairs, from every corner of the room!

The clock on the wall ground and whirred but couldn't strike the hour. Marie looked up and saw that the big golden owl that usually sat straight on top of the clock was hunched forward, its long beak jutting way out, its wings completely covering the hands and face. The clock's noisy gears continued to work until Marie could hear words in the pattern of the grinding:

> *Clocks, clocks, stop your ticking!*
> *Strike not, but sound this warning!*
> *The Mouse King hears you all.*
> *Prr prr, poom poom!*
> *He sings the age-old song of doom.*
> *Prr prr, poom poom!*
> *Bells, now chime!*
> *And so ring out the fated time!*

Then she heard the hoarse, smothered "poom" of the clock strike twelve.

Just as Marie was about to race out of the room, she spied Godpapa Drosselmeier on top of the clock! It wasn't the owl's wings at all but his scarlet coattails hanging down over the clock's face. "Godpapa," she called, "what are you doing up there? Come down, please! You're frightening me!"

But her godpapa didn't answer, and suddenly Marie heard a shrill squeaking and legions of tiny feet scurrying, while thousands of pinpoint lights glittered out through the cracks in the walls. It took Marie a moment to realize that the tiny lights were really eyes! Everywhere mice were peeping and squeezing themselves out through cracks all around the room. Group after group darted madly about, forming squadrons as neat and orderly as any Fritz had managed.

It was a good thing Marie was not afraid of mice, as many children are, for once the shock had passed, she found all their running around quite funny. But then a sound from somewhere close by sent a chill down her back. A sharp, terrible squeaking, and then—well, dear reader, all I can say is, even if you had all the

courage of our friend Field Marshal Fritz, you would have jumped into bed and pulled the covers up over your head if you'd seen what happened next. Our poor Marie, however, had no chance of escape, because the ground erupted at her feet, heaving up sand, lime, and broken stone. Out of the earth rose seven mouse heads with seven shiny crowns, all growing out of one large mouse body. Each head was hissing and squeaking so horribly that Marie had to cover her ears. Then all seven shouted in unison, calling the mouse army to gather before it. Marie's heart had been beating so fiercely that she thought she would die of fright, but now she felt as if her heart had stopped. Half-fainting, she fell back against the cupboard. Her elbow hit the glass front and one of the panes shattered, falling to the floor in splinters. There was a stinging in Marie's

arm, but she didn't mind it, because the awful squeaking had stopped. She thought that perhaps she had frightened the mice away—but still, she dared not look.

Meanwhile, right behind her, a great commotion started on the shelves of the cupboard, and small voices could be heard saying:

Awake and fight
For what is right!
Up now, away—
This is the night!

Glass harmonica bells tinkled so cheerfully that Marie found herself turning around to see who played them. Inside the cupboard, the tiny lamps were lit, and dolls along with other little figures hurried about, waving their arms. The Nutcracker threw off his blanket and leaped out of bed, shouting:

Knack knack knack,
Stupid mousey pack!
All their skulls we'll crack
Mousey pack, crick and crack—
Cowardly lot of schnack!

He drew his sword and held it in the air. "My loyal subjects and friends," he cried, "are you ready to stand beside me in this great battle?" Immediately, a clown named Scaramouche, one comical old man, four chimney sweeps, two zither players, and a drummer cried, "Yes, Your Highness! We, your loyal servants, will follow you to victory or death, come what may!" One after the other, they jumped down to the bottom shelf, their cotton insides and soft clothing affording them a safe landing. The fragile Nutcracker, however, would have broken something in the perilous leap if Miss Clara had not opened her arms and

received the hero, drawn sword and all, in her tender embrace. "Oh, Clara!" Marie cried. "How I misjudged you! You wanted to give your bed up to Nutcracker all along."

Miss Clara hugged the Nutcracker close and pleaded, "My lord, please do not fight this battle! You are wounded and sick, and your many followers are only too willing to fight in your place. Stay here with me and plan your victory from a safe distance." The Nutcracker, however, kicked impatiently until Clara let him go. When she released him, he sank down gracefully on one knee and said to her, "My lady, the kindness you have shown me will strengthen my heart for the battle to come." Clara bowed and, taking the Nutcracker by the arm, brought him to his feet. She then removed the beautiful spangled sash from her dress and tried to place it on his shoulders. But the little man stepped back and placed his hand on his heart. "My lady," he said, "I cannot wear your sash. You see..." He sighed, and holding up the ribbon which Marie had used as a bandage, he pressed it to his lips. Then, putting it about his shoulders, he brandished his sword and jumped out of the cupboard onto the floor.

You see, dear reader, even though the Nutcracker was made of wood, he felt and understood all of Marie's goodness and love; and out of his gratitude and devotion to her, he would not wear another's token, not even the glittering sash of Miss Clara. The Nutcracker prized the simple, unadorned ribbon that Marie had given him much much more.

When the Nutcracker hit the floor of the living room, the squeaking and piping started up louder than before. Under the big table that had earlier held Godpapa Drosselmeier's castle, hordes of mice formed huge battalions, awaiting orders from the terrible, seven-headed Mouse King. Where would it all end?

The Battle

"Begin the battle march, my trusty drummer!" cried the Nutcracker, and the drummer began to roll his drum so stirringly that the glass cupboard vibrated with the sound. Then all the lids for the boxes holding Fritz's army popped off, and soldiers climbed out and congregated on the bottom shelf to receive their orders. The Nutcracker made an inspection and then spoke to them of honor and courage. At the end of the speech, he looked about him.

"Why isn't the trumpeter sounding the call?" he shouted. He turned to old Pantaloon, who was quite pale, and said, "I know how brave and experienced you are, General!" His long chin wobbled as he spoke. "You're just the man I need to take charge! I hereby appoint you commander of the cavalry and artillery. Proceed on foot; your long legs can easily outrun a horse. And now, sir, to your duty!"

Immediately, Pantaloon put his bony fingers to his mouth and whistled more piercingly than any trumpet call, so that the cavalry and artillery divisions of Fritz's army came storming out, passing the Nutcracker in regiments with flags flying and bands playing. The artillery took their positions ahead of the cavalry and began firing. *Boom-boom!* Sugar plums shot out of rifles and catapults into the thickest part of the

mouse army. It wasn't long before considerable damage was evident in the enemy camp, where many heads were powdered white after a few rounds. The Nutcracker then ordered the biggest cannons into position on Mama's footstool, and *poom poom poom!*—a flying wall of gingerbread nuts blasted forth, toppling the mice in droves.

In spite of these efforts, the mouse army continued to advance upon the Nutcracker's men, using their heavy guns to best advantage. *Prr prr prr!* Marie could scarcely see through the smoke and dust of the battlefield. Nevertheless, she was certain that each soldier was fighting as hard and as bravely as he could. She watched for a long time, trying to figure out who would win.

The mice seemed to have endless numbers on their side. No sooner was one group hit than another would spring up in its place. They gathered the silver sprinkles from Christmas cakes, loaded their muskets with them, and fired at the glass cupboard, making the dolls inside fear for their lives. Clara and Gertrude ran up and down in a panic.

"I'm too young and beautiful to die like this!" cried Miss Clara.

"I've tried so hard to preserve my youthful looks all these years, only to be shot dead in my own drawing room! How tiresome!" Gertrude lamented.

They fell into each other's arms and wailed so miserably that Marie could hear them over the screams and weapon fire of battle. Amidst all the uproar—the *booroom booroom* of guns, the squeaking of the Mouse King, and the cries of the injured—Marie strained to hear the powerful voice of the Nutcracker in order to be sure he was all right.

Although General Pantaloon had distinguished himself with several brilliant cavalry charges, another division of Fritz's soldiers was assaulted with a foul-smelling pellet that stained their red tunics terribly. Pantaloon ordered them to lie low until they'd recovered. Unfortunately, this left the heavy artillery on Mama's footstool wide open to attack. In an instant, a large body of exceedingly ugly mice had launched an all-out assault, taking both guns and gunners in one fell swoop.

The Nutcracker was so alarmed by this that he ordered the right wing of his army to move back—which, as Field Marshal Fritz could tell you, is almost exactly the same as ordering a regular retreat. But never fear, dear reader! The Nutcracker's left wing was still fighting well and holding its ground.

During the worst of the fighting, masses of mouse cavalry had been quietly emerging from under the bureau, and now they rushed forward, squeaking horribly, at the Nutcracker's left wing. What a reception awaited them there! From out of the cupboard, over the treacherous ledge on the bottom shelf, came a regiment of china figures commanded by two Chinese emperors. As they formed orderly rows on the floor in front of the cabinet, it was apparent that the china squadron was indeed the most varied and brilliantly dressed of the day. There were Mongolians and Austrians, gardeners and hairdressers, harlequins and cupids, lions and tigers, unicorns and monkeys. They fought together with great courage and calm endurance. In fact, this elite battalion would surely have beaten the enemy if one of the mouse captains hadn't thrown himself at one of the Chinese emperors and bitten his head off. The emperor fell on his own troops, crushing the Mongolian sector and one of the unicorns. Sensing a weak spot, the enemy rushed in and bit the whole battalion to death! But this did them little good in the end, for soon all the mice who took part in this biting raid choked to death on bits of china caught in their throats.

Meanwhile, the Nutcracker's right wing had been suffering greater and greater losses and was now backed up against the wall.

"Bring up the reserves! Pantaloon! Scaramouche! Drummer! Where the devil are you?" shouted the Nutcracker, counting on reinforcements from the cupboard. The only ones left to join the battle, however, were the gingerbread men and women, who were so clumsy that they kept missing the enemy and bumping into their fellow fighters. Soon the mice found it easy to run up and bite off their gingerbread legs, causing them to fall over and crush still more of their comrades.

The Nutcracker was now surrounded by the enemy. He tried to climb the side of the cupboard but could not get a firm grip. Clara and Gertrude had fainted, so there was no one to give him a hand.

"A horse! A horse!" he shouted. "My kingdom for a horse!"

At that moment, two enemy riflemen seized him by his wooden cloak, and the Mouse King scurried over to him, squeaking in triumph out of all seven throats.

Marie was beside herself. "My poor Nutcracker!" she sobbed. Not knowing what else to do, she took her shoe off and threw it with all her might at the Mouse King.

Instantly, everything vanished. There was silence, and all traces of the horrible battle were gone. Marie felt the pain in her arm worsen before she passed out and fell to the floor in a dead faint.

The Invalid

When Marie awoke, she was lying in her own warm bed upstairs. The sun was shining on the window, where the night frost had left a pattern of flowers that shone silvery white. Marie heard someone say, "She's awake," and then her mother came in and looked at her anxiously. "Who is that man sitting by my bed?" Marie wondered, and then realized it was Dr. Wendelstern.

"Mama!" she whispered, "have all the mice left? Is Nutcracker all right?"

"What are talking about?" said her mother. "What have mice to do with the Nutcracker? We've been terribly worried about you, Marie. See what happens when you don't do as you're told? You were up so late with your toys that you fell asleep on the living room floor. You must have been frightened by a mouse and hit the glass cupboard with your elbow. Dr. Wendelstern removed all the splinters from your arm and said if they'd been any higher up, you might have bled to death! Thank heaven I went in to check on you around midnight and found you downstairs. You were bleeding terribly with all those toys around you, and one of your shoes was halfway across the room."

"Oh, Mama!" said Marie. "There was a big fight between the toys

and the mice. The mice were going to take Nutcracker prisoner, so I had to throw my shoe at them to save him."

Dr. Wendelstern looked at Marie's mother and gave her a little nod. She nodded back and then said to Marie: "It's all right, dear. Calm down, now. The mice are all gone, and Nutcracker is in the cupboard safe and sound." Then Marie's father came in for a long consultation with Dr. Wendelstern, who felt her pulse and said something to her father about "wound fever." She would have to stay in bed for a few days and take some medicine, even though she didn't feel very sick, except for her stiff arm. She was relieved that Nutcracker had escaped to safety, and seemed to remember, as if in a dream, that he'd turned to her and said, "Marie! Dearest lady! I am humbly in your debt. But you alone have the power to do even more for me." She tried to think of what this might mean but couldn't think of anything and fell asleep still wondering.

For the next few days, she wasn't allowed to play because of her arm, and when she tried to read or look at the pictures in her books, the print and the colors swam together before her eyes. So she had to wait until evening, when Mama would sit at her bedside and read to her. One evening, Mama had just finished telling her the story of a handsome prince, when the door opened and in came Godpapa Drosselmeier.

"I've come to see the invalid," he said, smiling.

Marie looked up and saw her godpapa wearing his long scarlet coat, and the whole scene of the awful battle came rushing back to her.

"Oh, Godpapa!" she said, "this is all your fault. I saw you keep the clock from striking and scaring the mice away. I heard you call the Mouse King. Why didn't you help Nutcracker? Why didn't you help *me*?"

Marie's mother asked her what she meant. But Drosselmeier made the oddest face and started to chant: "Pendulums could only rattle—couldn't tick, ne'er a tock. All the clocks stopped their ticking: no more clicking; then they all struck loud cling-clang. Dolls! Don't hang your heads so low! Cling and ring! The battle's over—Nutcracker's now all safe in clover. Comes the owl, on downy wing—Scares away the mouses' King. Pak and pik and pik and poom—pendulums must click again. Clocks, bim boom, grr grr."

31

Marie stared at Godpapa Drosselmeier, terrified. He looked more frightening than usual, and he was moving his right arm back and forth as if he were one of his mechanical men. Just when Marie thought she might die of fright, Fritz, who'd been watching from the door, laughed loudly and said, "Godpapa, you're so funny! You look just like one of my clowns!"

But their mother addressed Drosselmeier very seriously. "Why in the world are you carrying on like this?" she asked.

"What do you mean?" said Drosselmeier, laughing. "That's my Watchmaker's Song! I always sing it especially for little invalids like Marie." Then he sat down by Marie's bed and said, "Don't be angry with me for not gouging out the Mouse King's fourteen eyes. I couldn't manage it myself, but to make it up to you, I have a surprise I think you'll like."

He reached into one of his big pockets and slowly brought out—the Nutcracker! His teeth had all been put back in, and his jaw was set firm and straight. Marie shouted for joy, and her mother laughed and said, "Now you know how well Godpapa treats the Nutcracker."

"But Marie, you must admit," said her godpapa, "our Nutcracker is far from handsome. No one would ever mistake him for being good-looking. If you like, I'll tell you the story of how ugliness first came into his family, and why it is passed down to each generation."

Marie nodded, and her godpapa made himself a bit more comfortable in his chair.

"It all started with Princess Pirlipat, the witch Mouserink, and the clever clockmaker."

"I say, Godpapa Drosselmeier," interrupted Fritz. "Nutcracker's teeth are back in, but what's happened to his sword?"

Godpapa Drosselmeier shook his head. "You're always finding fault with something," he said irritably. "I've fixed his mouth, haven't I? He'll just have to find his own sword."

"I suppose so," said Fritz, with a shrug. "It is up to him, after all."

"So, Marie," continued Drosselmeier, "do you know the story of Princess Pirlipat?"

"No," said Marie, "could you tell it to me?"

"I hope it isn't as upsetting as your stories usually are," said Mama.

"Oh, no," said Drosselmeier. "On the contrary, it's quite amusing."

"Do tell us," cried Marie and Fritz. And he did.

The Story of the Hard Nut

irlipat was the daughter of a king and a queen, so naturally she was born a princess. The king was beside himself with joy at having such a beautiful daughter and danced about her cradle on one leg shouting, 'Hurray for my daughter! Has anyone ever seen a child as lovely as my Pirlipat?'

"The ministers of state, and the generals, the presidents, and other officials, all danced about on one leg too and cried, 'No, never!'

"It was true. There had never been a baby lovelier than Princess Pirlipat. Her little face could have been made of the most delicate white- and rose-colored silk. Her eyes were the clear blue of a summer sky, and her hair lay in gold ringlets all around her lovely head. What's more, she had come into the world with two perfect rows of pearly teeth, which she had already used to bite the finger of the lord high chancellor when he tried to inspect her features. 'My word!' he cried, wiping his finger on his handkerchief. (Some people insist that he really shouted 'Dear heaven!' but reports differ.) In any case, when everyone in the kingdom heard that little Pirlipat had bitten the lord high chancellor, they smiled, happy to know that intelligence and good taste were among the child's many fine qualities.

35

"Everything seemed perfect. The queen was uneasy, however, and had her daughter's cradle carefully guarded, though no one knew why. Not only were there guards at the door of the nursery, but two head nurses had to remain beside the cradle at all times, while six others were stationed about the room. Each of these nurses was ordered to keep a cat in her lap and to stroke it all night long, so it would never stop purring.

"Well, children, you couldn't possibly know why all these precautions were being taken, so I'll tell you.

"A long time ago, Pirlipat's father held a great festival in which many great rulers took part. Tournaments, theatricals, and state balls were planned, and the king spared no expense to make them very splendid indeed. After he had asked the court astronomer what would be the best time for pork butchering, he announced that there would be a great banquet of pudding and sausage to which all royal guests were invited. Then he went to the queen, bowed very low to her, and said, 'My darling, you are the only one who knows exactly how I like my pudding and sausage.' The queen smiled. She knew this was his way of asking her to prepare the food herself, and so she agreed. The chancellor of the exchequer was ordered to have the great golden sausage kettle and the silver casseroles taken out of the vault and sent to the kitchen. A fragrant sandalwood fire was kindled, and the queen donned her apron. Soon the most delicious aroma of pudding broth rose steaming out of the kettle. The enticing smell spread throughout the castle and into the council chamber, where the king, delighted by the aroma, was quite beside himself.

" 'Excuse me, my lords,' he said. 'I'll be back in a moment.' He leapt up and rushed to the kitchen, embraced the queen, and, after stirring the broth with his scepter, returned to the council chamber feeling much better.

"Next came the critical part of the whole recipe. The fat had to be cut up into little squares and browned on silver spits. The queen told her ladies-in-waiting to leave the kitchen for a while, as she wanted to do this part of the cooking herself out of love for her royal husband. As the fat began to brown, however, she heard a little voice say, 'Give me some of that. You're not the only queen in this castle. I want some too!' The queen knew instantly who it was: it was Dame Mouserink, ruler of Mousolia, who claimed relationship to the royal family and lived with her many subjects under the hearth. The queen was a kindhearted woman, and though she didn't think it proper to recognize Dame Mouserink as a sister, or a queen, she was quite willing to give her any tidbits she could spare. 'Come out, Dame Mouserink,' she said. 'You may taste the browned fat if you like.'

"Dame Mouserink hurried out, held up her grey paws, and swallowed the cubes of fat faster than the queen could feed them to her. Suddenly, all of Dame Mouserink's greedy relatives came scurrying out from the hearth, grabbing every piece of fat they could get hold of. Their greed so horrified the queen that she had no idea how to get rid of them. Fortunately, at that moment, the royal dressmaker entered the kitchen and drove the thieving little creatures away. What little fat was left had to be distributed among all of the hundreds of sausages. This was accomplished by a mathematical device capable of astonishingly small and precise measurements, so the sausages were ready in time for the great feast.

"Kettledrums and trumpets summoned princes and potentates alike. Each arrived at the palace in the finery of his native land. Some came in crystal carriages, others on the backs of pure white horses. The king received all of them graciously, then seated himself at the head of the banquet table. He raised his scepter and the feast began. First the white pudding was brought out, and right away the king knew there was something terribly wrong. Several of the guests noticed that he went very pale and lifted his eyes to heaven after just one mouthful. He sighed deeply, and it seemed as if some grave inner pain raged within him. Then the black puddings were served, and after one look at them, he fell back in his seat, sobbing pitifully.

"Everyone rose from the table as the court physician took the king's pulse. After the severest of remedies were administered—burnt feathers, castor oil, and the like—His Majesty recovered his senses enough to try and speak. With great effort he leaned forward and whispered the words 'Too little fat!' before collapsing back in his chair in bitter disappointment.

"The queen threw herself at his feet in despair and cried, 'Oh, my poor husband, what torture this is for you! I've hurt you terribly! Give me your worst punishment. For alas! Dame Mouserink, her seven sons, her uncles, cousins, and aunts, came and ate nearly all the fat, and—' At this point, the memory of the beastly crime made the queen fall back in a dead faint.

"On hearing this, the king jumped up in anger and shouted, 'Dressmaker, what is the meaning of this?'

"The royal dressmaker told all she knew, and the king decided to take revenge on Dame Mouserink and her family for eating the fat that should have gone into his sausages. The privy council was summoned, and it was resolved that Dame Mouserink should be put on trial for her life, and all her property confiscated. The king, however, knew that it would take a while for these proceedings to be arranged, and during that time Dame Mouserink would go on eating all the fat that belonged to him. So he

went to the court clockmaker—whose name was the same as your godpapa's, Christian Elias Drosselmeier—who assured the king he would expel Dame Mouserink and all her relations from the palace forever. To this end, the clockmaker invented a number of ingenious little contraptions containing pieces of browned fat and placed them around the dwelling of Dame Mouserink and her family. Now Mouserink herself was much too cunning to fall for this sort of thing and warned all her relatives not to go near the fat, but it was no use. All her seven sons and many of her uncles, aunts, and cousins couldn't resist the temptation and so walked right into Drosselmeier's traps. As soon as they set foot inside, where the browned fat was, a metal bar snapped shut behind them, making them prisoners, after which they met with a shameful death in the kitchen.

"Dame Mouserink, filled with rage and sadness, left the castle, vowing revenge. Everyone at court rejoiced at finally being rid of her—everyone, that is, except the queen, who knew Dame Mouserink would find a way to avenge the death of her family. Indeed, not too long after that, it so happened that the queen was cooking fricassee of sheep's eyes—a favorite delicacy of the king's—when Dame Mouserink appeared before her and said, 'My sons and uncles and cousins and aunts are gone because of you! Watch your step, or the queen of mice will bite your pretty daughter in two!'

"With this, she vanished. The queen was so shaken that she dropped the fricassee into the fire. And so yet another of the king's favorite dishes was spoiled by Dame Mouserink, which, as you can imagine, did not make him very happy.

"But that's enough for tonight," said Godpapa Drosselmeier. "I'll continue the story another time."

Marie, who had her own ideas about the story, begged Godpapa Drosselmeier to go on, but he wouldn't be persuaded and told the children that too much of it at once would not be good for them, and they would hear the rest tomorrow.

Just as Drosselmeier was leaving, Fritz said, "By the way, Godpapa, was it really you who invented mousetraps?"

"Don't be so silly, Fritz," said his mother. But Drosselmeier laughed and, with a strange twinkle in his eye, answered, "Well, you know, I *can* make clocks, and mousetraps had to be invented by someone."

"So now you know," continued Godpapa Drosselmeier the following evening, "why the queen took such pains to ensure the safety of her little Pirlipat. The fear of Dame Mouserink's returning to bite her daughter to death was always with her. And Drosselmeier's mouse catchers were of no use against the clever Mouserink. The court astronomer, however, claimed that members of the Cat Purr family would keep her away. So each of Pirlipat's nurses was given a cat—and all of the cats were given the official title "Officer of the Law"—which she was obliged to keep awake in her lap day and night.

"One night, however, the head nurse, who had dropped off into a sound sleep, woke with a start. The whole house seemed buried in a slumber as silent as death, with not a single purr to be heard. Suddenly, she saw a huge, ugly mouse poised on its hind legs, bending over the cradle, laying its disgusting head on the princess's face! She sprang out of her chair with a scream that woke the entire household. Dame Mouserink ran to a corner of the room. The Officers of the Law meowed and hurried after her— but it was too late! She had already escaped through a crack in the floor. The noise woke and frightened little Pirlipat, and she started to cry.

" 'Thank heaven she's alive!' said the nurses, but when they went over to check on her, their mouths fell open. Instead of a delicate little golden head, they saw an enormous bloated one atop a tiny, crumpled body. Where there once had been a beautiful pair of blue eyes, now there were green, lifeless ones without sparkle. Her mouth, which had once been so dainty, now stretched ridiculously from one side of her huge head to the other.

"The queen nearly died of sorrow. The castle shook with her heart-rending sobs. And the walls of the king's study had to be padded because he kept banging his head against them, crying, 'How wretched I am!' You would have thought it only natural for him to consider how much better things might've been if he'd settled for puddings without fat and let Dame Mouserink and her family alone. But he didn't. Instead, he blamed the court clockmaker, Christian Elias Drosselmeier, and issued an edict ordering him to restore his daughter to her former beauty—or at least find out how it could be done—in four weeks' time, or be beheaded.

"Drosselmeier was terrified. Immediately, he tried taking the princess apart, unscrewing her hands and feet, to examine her interior structure. What he found was disastrous. He realized that the older the princess grew, the more deformed she would become, and not even his vast technical skills could correct her condition. He put her together again and sank down next to her cradle, filled with despair.

"On Wednesday of the fourth week, the king, eyes gleaming with anger, approached his clockmaker and said, 'Christian Elias Drosselmeier, restore the princess to health or prepare to die!'

"Drosselmeier began to weep bitterly. The little princess kept on cracking nuts, which seemed to be the only thing that made her happy. It dawned on the clockmaker that it was quite extraordinary that Pirlipat not only had been born with teeth but had cried terribly after her transformation until given a nut, which she had immediately cracked. After popping the kernel in her mouth, she was quiet. From then on, the nurses gave her nuts to keep her calm.

" 'O wise and subtle nature! O mysterious interdependence of things!' cried Drosselmeier. 'You're showing me the door to the cure of the princess's illness. I will knock, and it will be opened to me.'

"He immediately asked for an interview with the court astronomer and was taken to him under heavy guard. They embraced tearfully and went to a private room where there were books on treatments, spells, charms, and other mysterious subjects. When it grew dark, the court astronomer consulted the stars and, with Drosselmeier's help, charted the princess's horoscope. At first it seemed only a hopeless jumble of lines, but after many hours they were rewarded with the key to ending Pirlipat's bewitchment. All the princess had to do to regain her former beauty was to eat the sweet kernel of the Crackatook nut.

"Now the Crackatook nut had a shell so hard that you could fire a cannon at it without even making a dent. Furthermore, to break the spell, the nut had to be cracked in front of the princess by a man who'd never shaved or worn boots. After cracking the nut, this man was to hand the kernel to the princess with his eyes closed and, keeping them closed, take seven steps backward without tripping.

"The night before Drosselmeier was to be executed, he burst into the castle dining room, where the king was having dinner, and announced he had found the way to restore the princess to her natural beauty. The king leapt from the table and hugged the clockmaker, promising him a diamond sword, four medals, and two Sunday suits.

" 'Get to work right after dinner,' the king said, adding with a wink, 'Be sure the young man doesn't have anything to drink before his seven steps backward. He can drink all he wants when it's over!'

"However, Drosselmeier explained to the king that both the young man and the Crackatook nut had to be searched for, and that there was a possibility that they wouldn't be found at all. The king waved his scepter over his crowned head and roared, 'In that case, I'll have you beheaded now!'

"Fortunately for Drosselmeier, the king had greatly enjoyed his dinner and so was inclined to listen to the queen, who took pity on the clockmaker and intervened on his behalf. Drosselmeier pointed out that he had already met the conditions set down by His Majesty by discovering how to cure the princess. The king disagreed. After a few glasses of port, however, he softened and ordered the clockmaker and astronomer to begin the search, warning that they were not to return without the Crackatook nut safely in hand. The queen suggested they advertise in newspapers far and wide to find the youth who would crack the legendary nut."

And with that, Godpapa Drosselmeier told Marie it was time for her to go to sleep and that he'd finish the story the next evening.

The next day, as soon as the evening lamps had been lit, Godpapa Drosselmeier arrived and continued the story. "The clockmaker and the court astronomer had been journeying for fifteen years without finding a single trace of the Crackatook nut. It would take another four weeks, children, to tell you of all the extraordinary places they'd been and things they'd seen, so we won't go into it. I can tell you, though, that after fifteen years, Drosselmeier the clock-maker felt a deep yearning to see his hometown of Nuremberg once more. One day, his homesickness was worse than usual; and suddenly, while smoking a pipe in the middle of some Asian forest with his friend the astronomer, he cried out:

Oh, Nuremberg, Nuremberg, my hometown,
Those who don't know you, place of renown,
Though far they may travel, and great cities see—
London and Paris and Peterwardein—
They know not how happy and sweet home can be,
And so our hearts ache and dream sadly of thee.

"The astronomer was seized with such compassion upon hearing his friend grieve that he wept and lamented so loudly, he was heard all across Asia. When he'd regained his composure, he wiped the tears from his eyes and said, 'Why be miserable here? Let's go to Nuremberg! We may as well look there for the horrible nut as anywhere else.'

" 'You are right,' said Drosselmeier. So they got up, knocked the ashes out of their pipes, and started home. As soon as they arrived, Drosselmeier went straight to his cousin the toymaker, whom he hadn't seen for years, and told him the whole story of Princess Pirlipat, Dame Mouserink, and the nut Crackatook. The toymaker clapped his hands, amazed, and said, 'My dear cousin, how marvelous!'

"Then Drosselmeier told him about their travels: how he had spent two years at the court of the King of Dates, how the Prince of Almonds had thrown him out of his kingdom, and how he had applied without success to the Historical Society at Squirreltown—in other words, how he had looked high and low for the Crackatook nut and hadn't found it anywhere.

"While he was talking, Christoph Zacharias, the toymaker, kept hopping up and down in his chair. 'Oh, my,' he cried, 'how very extraordinary!' Suddenly he stood up, threw his wig in the air, and embraced his cousin. 'Cousin, cousin! Your search is over! I have the Crackatook nut right here!' He took out a little carved wooden box, opened it, and showed Drosselmeier a medium-sized nut that had been carefully gilded.

" 'You see,' he said, turning the nut in his hand, 'several Christmases ago, a stranger came to my house with a bag of nuts and offered to sell them. He got into a row just in front of my house with some nut sellers and put his sack down in the road. A carriage ran over it, and all the nuts were smashed but this one. He offered it to me at a price that turned out to be exactly the amount of money I happened to have in my pocket. I don't know why I took the trouble to gild it; I imagine it just struck my fancy.'

"Drosselmeier wondered if this could really be the very nut he had been searching for all this time, but then the astronomer scraped away the gilding and found the word 'Crackatook' written on the shell in Chinese. The exiled pair danced for joy, and their cousin danced too, for Drosselmeier assured him that his fortune was made, and from then on he would see to it that the toymaker had an unlimited supply of gold leaf for his work at no charge.

"That night, as the clockmaker and the astronomer put on their nightcaps for bed, the astronomer said, 'You know, good luck doesn't come in a single dose. I'm almost certain we've found not only the nut for the princess but the young man to crack it as well—your cousin's son. I'm not going to sleep until I chart that boy's horoscope.' He threw off his nightcap and went to work consulting the stars.

"The stars revealed that the boy was handsome and strong, had never shaved, and had never worn boots. True, in his awkward growing years he had played a Jumping Jack in a holiday pageant. But now he was past all that. His father had taken every care with him and just last Christmas had given him a beautiful red coat trimmed in gold, with hat to match, not to mention a sword and a fine wig with a pigtail. The boy had stood in his father's shop wearing his new clothes and cracking nuts. He was much admired by the young ladies who'd stopped by, and they dubbed him 'the handsome nutcracker.'

"In the morning, the astronomer took Drosselmeier by the hand and cried, 'We've found him! The very one! But listen, dear cousin, there are two things we must do. First, we must strengthen the boy's pigtail and connect it to his jaw to make his bite more powerful. And second, when we return to the palace, we must keep him a secret for a while. His horoscope says that if two or three others try to crack the nut and fail, the king will promise not only his daughter's hand in marriage but also his crown to the one who succeeds!'

"The toymaker was delighted at the idea of his son marrying the princess and becoming king, so he entrusted the boy to his cousin and the astronomer. Drosselmeier attached a pigtail to the boy, and then tested its efficiency by having him crack some extremely tough peach stones, which he did with great ease. Then the clockmaker sent word to the palace of their impending arrival with the Crack-atook nut and placed an advertisement in the local papers for a young man to crack it. By the time our travelers entered the palace, there was a line of fine young gentlemen, some of them princes, awaiting their turn to disenchant the princess.

"Drosselmeier and his friend were horrified when they saw Pirlipat again. Her petite body with its tiny hands and feet was nowhere near big enough to support her big, shapeless head. Her face too, already hideous, had become even worse because of the white beard that had grown up about her mouth and chin.

"Everything the court astronomer had seen in the horoscope came true. One young man after another took the nut and bit into it as hard as he could until his teeth wobbled and his jaw ached and he was carried out of the chamber by a team of physicians. It was difficult for the young men to talk after their ordeal, but each one could be heard trying to say, '*That* certainly was a hard nut to crack!' or something similar, as they were escorted to medical attention.

"Just as the astronomer had predicted, the king grew so anxious over the many failures to crack the nut that he announced that the man who succeeded should have his daughter's hand in marriage and rule the kingdom. Just then, the clockmaker's nephew, young Drosselmeier, stepped up and asked to be given a chance. He was by far the handsomest to come forward, and when the princess saw him, she pressed her hands to her heart and said, 'I hope *he* will be my husband.'

"After politely saluting the queen and Princess Pirlipat, young Drosselmeier took the nut from the princess, put it between his teeth, and lo and behold—the shell split open and fell to the floor. He picked the kernel out of the pieces of husk that stuck to it and went down on one knee before the princess, holding it out to her. The princess accepted the

nut, and the young man began his seven steps backward. Pirlipat popped the kernel into her mouth and swallowed it. Everyone rubbed their eyes and stared as the monstrosity that Pirlipat had been faded away into a beautiful young lady whose complexion seemed woven of delicate lily-white and rose-red silk, and whose eyes shone like a summer sky. Pirlipat looked down at herself, and her own golden curls fell about her lovely face.

"Trumpets and kettledrums mingled with the cheerful rejoicing of the people. The king and his court all danced about on one leg, as they had at the princess's birth. The queen fainted from sheer joy and had to be given a whiff of eau de cologne to bring her around. All this commotion distracted young Drosselmeier somewhat; but, keeping his composure, he stretched out his right foot to take the seventh step backward. Alas, before his heel could settle on the floor, Dame Mouserink came up through the floorboards, squeaking horribly, and ran under his foot so that he stumbled and nearly fell. When he had regained his balance, his appearance was completely transformed. He was just as grotesque as the princess had been under Dame Mouserink's spell: his body was shriveled and couldn't support his great shapeless head with its enormous popping eyes, and wide, gaping mouth. And where his handsome pigtail had been, there was only a thin wooden cloak which guided the movement of his lower jaw.

"The clockmaker and the astronomer were horrified, but then they saw that Dame Mouserink's wickedness had been punished, for she was mortally wounded in the throat and languished where young Drossel-meier's foot had crushed her. Writhing in pain, she cried:

> *O Crackatook, you nut so hard!*
> *O fate, which none may disregard!*
> *A final spell on you I cry,*
> *Since I through that hard nut must die*
> *The brave young Nutcracker, you will see,*
> *Will die and follow after me.*
> *My own sweet son with seven crowns*
> *Will surely bring Nutcracker down.*

49

In horrid death I curse your life
No princess here will be your wife!

"With that, Dame Mouserink squeaked a final time and died. Her body was carried out and disposed of by the court stovelighter.

"With all that had happened, no one had noticed the startling transformation of young Drosselmeier. However, when the princess reminded the king of his promise, and the young man was brought before her, she could not believe her eyes. Covering her face at the sight of him, she cried, 'Please, please, take that horrible creature away!' The lord chamberlain seized the Nutcracker and threw him out of the palace, while the king, furious that a nutcracker should be brought to him as a suitable son-in-law, blamed everything on the clockmaker and astronomer and ordered them banished forever.

"The astronomer had not seen anything like this in the horoscope he had charted in Nuremberg, so he decided to cast it again for fresh information. The stars told him that despite Dame Mouserink's spell, young Drosselmeier would behave so admirably that he would still be a prince, and then a king. However, his deformity would vanish only if he was able to destroy the seven-headed Mouse King, the son born to Dame Mouserink after the death of her first seven sons, and win the heart of a lady in spite of his ugliness.

"And that," said Godpapa Drosselmeier, "is the story of the Crackatook nut. Now you know why people use the expression 'That was a hard nut to crack,' and why nutcrackers are so ugly."

Marie thought Princess Pirlipat was mean and ungrateful. Fritz, on the other hand, said that if he were in the Nutcracker's shoes, he would do away with the Mouse King in no time and get his good looks back too.

Uncle and Nephew

If you, dear reader, have ever been cut by glass, you know what a nasty business it is and how long it takes to heal. Marie had to stay in bed a whole week to get her strength back. After that, she was as good as new and couldn't wait to see her new toys looking shiny and magical in the glass cupboard. Best of all, she was reunited with her dear Nutcracker, who smiled at her from the second shelf with all his teeth. She looked at him fondly and suddenly realized that Godpapa Drosselmeier's story had been about her Nutcracker and his family feud with Dame Mouserink and her people. Of course! Her Nutcracker was none other than young Drosselmeier of Nuremberg, her godpapa's nephew, under the spell of Dame Mouserink! Why else would she have felt during the telling of the story that the clockmaker was Godpapa Drosselmeier himself?

Marie felt a tug at her heart. "Why didn't your uncle help you?" she whispered, tears filling her eyes. She now understood that the battle she had witnessed was the Nutcracker's attempt to regain his crown and kingdom. Yes, she thought, all the other toys were his subjects, weren't they? The astronomer's prophecy about the Nutcracker being the true King of Toyland had come true.

While Marie weighed these things in her mind, she watched the Nutcracker and the others closely for signs of life—a small wave or a blink of an eye perhaps. But not one of them moved. Everything in the cupboard stayed perfectly still. They're under Dame Mouserink's spell, Marie thought, and, touching the cupboard lightly, she said, "That's all right, my dear Mr. Drosselmeier. I know you understand me and how much I care for you. You can always rely on my help whenever you need it, and I shall ask your uncle to help you too."

The Nutcracker remained quiet, but Marie imagined a gentle sigh coming through the glass, and a pure, bell-like voice singing:

Marie, fine, angel mine!
I will be yours if you will be mine!

Although Marie felt a cold shiver go through her, it gave her the greatest pleasure.

At twilight, Louise laid out the tea table, and the family gathered around it and began talking about all sorts of things, the way families do. Marie put her small chair at her godpapa's feet; and when there was a lull in the conversation, she looked straight at him with her blue eyes and said, "Now I know, Godpapa, that the Nutcracker is your nephew from Nuremberg. The prophecy has come true. He is a king and a prince just like your friend the astronomer said he'd be. And we both know he's at war with Dame Mouserink's son, that horrible king of the mice. So why don't you help him?"

Marie told them all about the battle she'd seen, and though her mother and sister frequently interrupted her with their laughter, Fritz and Drosselmeier listened carefully to Marie's every word. When she'd finished, her father leaned back in his chair and turned to her mother.

"Where does she get such nonsense?" he cried.

"She has a lively imagination," said her mother. "She dreamed it all when she was feverish with her arm."

"I don't believe it," said Fritz. "My soldiers are not cowards! I wouldn't command them if they were!"

But Godpapa Drosselmeier smiled strangely, took Marie on his knee, and spoke more gently to her than he ever had before.

"More has been revealed to you, Marie," he said, "than to me or any of the others. You are a born princess, like Pirlipat, and reign in a beautiful country. But you have a rough road ahead of you if you want to befriend the Nutcracker. The Mouse King waits for him at every turn. I cannot help him. You are the only one who can. So be faithful and true."

Marie didn't really understand what her godpapa meant, and, of course, neither did the others. In fact, Dr. Stahlbaum was so perplexed by Drosselmeier's behavior that he went over and took his pulse, saying, "Your head must be congested. I'd better write you a prescription."

But Marie's mother, who'd grown quiet when Drosselmeier spoke, shook her head thoughtfully and said, "I think I know what Godpapa Drosselmeier means, though I can't quite put in into words."

Victory

One moonlit night shortly thereafter, Marie awoke to the sound of someone throwing small stones in a corner of her bedroom. She heard them fall and roll across the floor, followed by a shrill squeaking.

"Oh, dear," she cried. "It's those awful mice again!" Marie wanted to run and wake up her mother, but when she saw the King of the Mice squeezing himself through a hole in the wall, she froze in her bed. Once he'd pushed his whole ugly body through the crack in the wall, the Mouse King ran around the room and then jumped up on Marie's bedside table.

"Hee-hee-hee," he cried, "give me your candy! Quick as you can. I want your cakes, and your marzipan, and your gingerbread men! Now do as I tell you, because if you don't, I'll chew up your Nutcracker! See if I don't!"

Marie could not take her eyes from his sharp teeth, which were gnashing and chattering horribly. Even after he had scurried back into the hole in the wall, she couldn't get them out of her mind, and so she was awake most of the night. In the morning, her mother remarked that she looked pale, and Marie yearned to tell her about the awful threats of the Mouse King; but she held her tongue, fearing her mother would only

laugh and say she had
been dreaming.

Nonetheless, Marie
knew that to protect the
Nutcracker, she would
have to give up all her
sweets. That night, before
she went to bed, she
gathered them to-
gether and
spread them
out in front
of the cupboard. Sure enough, the next morning, most of the sweets were entirely eaten,
with only a few crumbs left. Even the marzipan,
which the Mouse King had evidently not found to
his liking, had been chewed around the edges so that
whatever remained would have to be thrown out. Still,
Marie didn't really mind losing her candy when she
thought of how it had saved the Nutcracker. The next
night, however she awoke to a loud squeaking in her
ear, only to find the King of Mice glaring at her more
viciously than before.

"Give me your sugar toys," he demanded. "Give them you must, or
watch me chew Nutcracker up into dust!" Then he vanished.

Marie grew very sad. She had as beautiful a collection of white- and
maple-sugar toys as any child could wish for. Not only did she have a
little shepherd and a shepherdess with their flock of milk-white sheep
and a cheerful dog that jumped around them, but she also had a pair of
mailmen carrying letters, and several beautifully dressed young gentlemen and ladies seated in a Russian swing. There were dancers too, and a
farmer, but Marie didn't care too much about *them*. In the back of the
cupboard, however, in the corner, was a rosy-cheeked infant, and *this* was
Marie's favorite. When she thought of this darling being eaten by the
Mouse King, she started to cry.

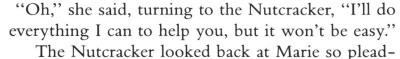

"Oh," she said, turning to the Nutcracker, "I'll do everything I can to help you, but it won't be easy." The Nutcracker looked back at Marie so pleadingly that she made up her mind to sacrifice every one of the sugar toys. She remembered the Mouse King's seven sets of grinding teeth and quickly arranged the little figures in front of the cupboard in the same spot as before. She kissed the shepherd and shepherdess and placed the darling baby a little farther back than the rest, leaving the front for the farmer and a few of the dancers.

The next morning, Marie's mother found the mess in the drawing room and shook her head. "What a shame! A mouse must have made a hole in the glass cupboard and taken your sugar toys. They're all over the floor, gnawed to bits." Marie couldn't hold back her tears at first, but soon she dried them, reminding herself that the Nutcracker was safe.

That evening, Marie's mother told Father and Godpapa about the damage to the things in the glass cupboard.

"What a nuisance," said her father. "We should get rid of that blasted mouse before it ruins all the children's toys."

"*I* know!" said Fritz. "The baker downstairs has a grey cat who'll bite the head off of any mouse—even Dame Mouserink and her ugly son."

"Yes," his mother said. "And it will claw the drapes and jump on the furniture and knock over lamps and glasses."

"Oh no, Mama," said Fritz. "The baker's cat is really clever. I wish I could walk around the edge of the roof the way he does."

"Please no cats in the house at night! I won't be able to sleep," said Louise, who hated cats.

"Fritz's idea is a good one," said their mother. "Or we could set a trap. Do we have one in the house?"

"Godpapa Drosselmeier is the man to ask," said Fritz. "He invented them." Everybody laughed; but, sure enough, when their mother asked Drosselmeier about it, he said he had plenty and brought one over to the house the same day.

As the cook was browning fat for the trap, Marie, whose head was filled with her godpapa's story, shouted, "Watch out, Queen! Remember Dame Mouserink and her people." Whereupon Fritz drew his wooden sword and said, "I dare them to show their faces! Leave them to me!" But the hearth was quiet. Drosselmeier threaded the browned fat on a fine piece of wire and then set it in the glass cupboard.

"Godpapa!" called Fritz. "Be careful the Mouse King doesn't trick you!" But Godpapa did not answer.

That night, Marie felt something icy cold crawl up her arm, and something rough and scratchy brush across her cheek. Then she heard a squeaking in her ear. It was the Mouse King sitting on her shoulder with blood-red foam spilling out of all his seven mouths. He hissed into Marie's ear:

> *Hiss! Hiss!*
> *Traps are set!*
> *Inside the house!*
> *Awake! Awake!*
> *Your orders take*
> *From me, King Mouse*
> *Give up your books with pictures fine.*
> *Your laces, dresses*
> *Now are mine!*
> *Watch your step or else I'll chew*
> *Your Nutcracker in pieces two!*
> *Fee-fie-foe-fum*
> *His funeral day has finally come.*
> *Hee-hee-hee. Squeak, squeak!*

Marie arose the next morning looking ill and unhappy. Mrs. Stahlbaum thought she was troubled over the loss of her sugar toys and hugged her daughter tightly.

"Don't worry, dear," she said. "If the mousetraps don't work, we'll have Fritz bring up the baker's cat."

After her mother had left the room, Marie went over to the glass cupboard to look in on the Nutcracker. "My dear, sweet Mr. Drossel-meier," she sobbed, "what can I do? Even if I give the Mouse King all my picture books and the new dress the Christ Child brought me for Christmas, he'll still want more. Soon I won't have anything left, and he'll want to eat *me*! What shall I do?"

As she finished crying, she noticed a spot of blood on the Nutcracker's neck from the night of the great battle. And even though she had stopped carrying him around and hugging him since she'd found out he was really her godpapa's nephew, she took him delicately off the shelf and wiped off the spot of blood with her handkerchief. No sooner had she started to attend to his wound than the Nutcracker grew warm, then warmer, and began to move! Quickly, she set him back down on the cupboard shelf and looked on, trembling, as his bearded chin began to wobble backward and forward.

"Dear Miss Stahlbaum, most precious of friends. I am indebted to you for everything—everything!" he said. "But please don't sacrifice any of your picture books or pretty dresses for me. All I need is a sword. If you can get me a sword, I'll do the rest ... though ... my enemy. ..." The Nutcracker's voice faded, and his eyes, which had been so warm and compassionate, became lifeless and wooden once again. But Marie wasn't afraid; she jumped for joy now that she knew how to help her Nutcracker without losing the rest of her lovely things. but where would she get a sword? She decided to ask Fritz; and that evening when their father and mother went out, she stood next to her brother by the glass cupboard and told him what had happened to her, and about the Nutcracker and the King of the Mice, and what she needed to rescue the Nutcracker once and for all. Fritz asked Marie if his soldiers had really behaved so badly in the great battle, and Marie assured him on her honor she was telling the truth. Fritz nodded in understanding and then turned to his soldiers. He spoke plainly and movingly to his men, explaining that, as punishment, they would have to forfeit their plumes and refrain from sounding the official marching call for twelve months. When he had finished, Fritz turned to Marie and said,

"As for a sword, I can help. I retired one of my colonels yesterday, so he won't need his sword anymore. It's a good one too."

The colonel was settled comfortably in the back corner of the third shelf. Fritz took him out and removed his saber, which he then secured on the Nutcracker. That night, Marie lay wide awake with anticipation and fear. Around midnight, she thought she heard a noise in the sitting room—a rustling and then a clanging—and then, much louder, a shrill squeak.

"The King of Mice! The King of Mice!" she cried, jumping out of bed in terror. Not knowing what action to take, Marie kept very still until she heard a gentle tapping on her door and a soft voice say, "Please open your door, Miss Stahlbaum. Don't be afraid. I have good news!"

It was the voice of young Drosselmeier. Marie threw on her dressing gown and opened the door. There was the Nutcracker, holding his bloodied sword in one hand and a candle in the other. When he saw Marie, he went down on one knee and said, "It was you, and you alone, dear lady, who gave me the courage and strength to fight the insolent creature who dared to insult you. The Mouse King lies dying and will never bother you again. Please accept these tokens of victory from your true and faithful knight." He handed the seven tiny crowns of the Mouse King to Marie, who received them joyfully. The Nutcracker then stood up and said, "My beloved, I have wonderful things to show you! Do, please, come with me!"

Toyland

I'm certain, children, that you wouldn't have hesitated for a moment to go with the Nutcracker, who'd proven to be such a good fellow. Marie was all the more inclined to follow him because she knew he was filled with gratitude for all her help. So she said, "Of course I'll go with you, dear Mr. Drosselmeier. But not very far and not for too long. I need to get some rest."

"Then we'll take the shortest route," replied the Nutcracker, "though it's probably the most difficult."

He led Marie to the big old wardrobe. She was surprised to see that it was wide open, with her father's traveling coat hanging right in front. The Nutcracker took hold of the hem and climbed up along the edge of the fox trim until he arrived at a big tassel fastened at the shoulder of the coat. He gave the tassel a tug and a pretty little cedar ladder came down from one of the sleeves.

"Now, Miss Stahlbaum, if you would be so kind as to step up the ladder," said the Nutcracker. And so she did. As soon as she'd gotten as far up as the neck of the coat, however, a dazzling light poured over her, and she found herself in a sweet-smelling meadow which glittered like millions of beautiful gems.

"This is Candy Meadow," the Nutcracker explained. "Come. Let's go through that gate there."

Marie looked up and saw a lovely gate a few steps away. It seemed at first to be made of white, brown, and raisin-colored marble, but as she drew closer, she realized it was made of baked sugar almonds and raisins. The Nutcracker called it Almond Raisin Gate and pointed out a walkway running along the top of it, where six monkeys in little red suits played trumpets and French horns. The road they were on was made of pieces of multicolored hard candies of every flavor. It led to a forest that was fragrant with the scent of oranges. Beautiful ribbons hung from the trees, and every branch was heavy with gold and silver fruits. A gentle breeze stirred the forest, so the glittering tinsel ribbons rustled like beautiful music, as light danced off the fruit of the swaying branches.

"How very charming!" said Marie, entranced.

"Dear Miss Stahlbaum," said the Nutcracker, "this is Christmas Wood."

"Oh," said Marie, "if only I could stay here a little while. It's *so* lovely."

The Nutcracker clapped his hands, and immediately shepherds and shepherdesses molded of white sugar appeared from a different part of the wood. They brought out a gold reclining chair with a white satin cushion and invited Marie to sit down. As soon as Marie was comfortable, the shepherds and shepherdesses performed a ballet for her and then disappeared back into the forest.

"I apologize for the poor quality of the dance, my dear Miss Stahlbaum," said the Nutcracker. "Our Wind-up Ballet Troupe can only do the same steps over and over again. Let's go on a little farther."

"But I thought it was lovely," said Marie. "Really." She stood up and followed the Nutcracker along a rippling brook. The scent of oranges was even stronger and sweeter here.

"This is Orange Brook," said the Nutcracker. "Its scent is sweet, but the waters of River Lemonade are far more beautiful. Both streams run into the Almond Milk Sea. Come, I'll show you."

As they crested the next hill, Marie heard the sound of rushing water, and, looking down, she saw the large rolling swells of the River

Lemonade. A cool freshness blew across her cheeks, gladdening her heart. Nearby was a slow, narrower stream, where children sat on the banks, scooping up the little round fishes that swam in its waters. As Marie approached, she saw the fish were really hazelnuts and that up ahead was a little village, whose golden-brown buildings were decorated with lemon peel and shelled almonds.

"This is Gingertown on the Honey River," said the Nutcracker. "The inhabitants are very good-looking, but they suffer from such painful toothaches that they're usually quite cranky. We'll come back another time."

A short distance away, Marie could see a cluster of houses that seemed to be made of multicolored sheets of glass. The Nutcracker led the way into the town, where a crowd of pleasant little people were busy unloading tiny packages of colored paper and tablets of chocolate from a long line of wagons.

"This is Bonbonville," the Nutcracker said. "Supplies have just arrived from Paperland and the King of Chocolate. These poor citizens have been repeatedly threatened by the Fly Admiral's forces, so they're covering their homes with special-issue sticky sheets from Paperland. But forgive me, Miss Stahlbaum. I won't bore you any longer with the small towns and villages. It's high time you saw the capital."

He proceeded quickly and Marie followed, full of anticipation. A rosy mist began to cover the land around them, giving everything a soft splendor. Marie saw that the mist was reflected in the stream that gurgled alongside them, flowing out toward the horizon, where it widened into a lake with waves of red and silver. On these waters, white swans with collars of gold floated gracefully by, singing to them, while fish which glittered like diamonds danced over the rosy waves.

"Oh, my!" said Marie. "I know what this is. It's the lake Godpapa was going to make for me so that I could play with the swans!'"

The Nutcracker smiled scornfully and laughed in a way that Marie had never seen before. "I doubt it," he said. "My uncle could never make a lake like this. You could, Marie, if you wanted to. But let's not worry about that now. It's time to sail over Lake Rosa to the city."

The Capital of Toyland

The Nutcracker clapped his hands and the waves of Lake Rosa grew higher. As Marie watched, a carriage made of precious stones approached, pulled by two dolphins with scales of gold. Then twelve beautiful Nubian boys with headdresses and jackets made of hummingbirds' feathers jumped ashore and led Marie and the Nutcracker into the shell-shaped carriage, which then moved through the water of its own accord. In the wake of the dolphins, water shot up into the air and came down in a sparkling rain that seemed to say in a chorus of tiny voices,

> *Who comes over the rosy sea? Fairy is she.*
> *Fishes and swans, awake and sing. Sparkle and ring.*
> *Here is the fairy we've longed to see,*
> *Coming at last to us over the sea.*
> *Rosy waves dash, bright dolphins speed. Merrily, merrily on!*

But the twelve boys at the back of the car had their own song, and they shook the palm leaves they were holding and stamped their feet and sang:

NUTCRACKER

Klapp and klipp, klipp and klapp,
Down and up, up and down.

"These fellows are quite amusing," said the Nutcracker. "But they'll probably set the whole lake in an uproar, and then where will we be?"

Indeed, they noticed a great confusion of strange voices floating in the water and in the air around them. Marie paid no attention to the feuding songs but continued to gaze at the rosy waters, where she saw the beautiful face of a young girl smiling up at her from every wave.

"Look, Mr. Drosselmeier," she said, pointing into the water. "There's Princess Pirlipat smiling back at me!"

The Nutcracker sighed deeply and said, "That is not Princess Pirlipat, dear Miss Stahlbaum. It's you. That is your own lovely reflection you see in the waves."

Marie, who was terribly embarrassed, instantly shut her eyes and leaned back in her seat. But then the twelve little boys lifted her out of the water carriage and set her down on shore. When she opened her eyes, she found herself in a grove even more beautiful than Christmas Wood. The fruits on the trees were extraordinary and wonderful, and an enticing fragrance surrounded her.

"Ah! Here we are in Sugar Plum Grove, and there's the capital."

Dear reader, how can I begin to describe all the wonderful things Marie saw here, or give you any idea of the magnificence of the city that rose up before her on a flowery plain? The walls and towers shimmered with different colors, and the shapes of the buildings were like nothing Marie had ever seen. Instead of a roof, each house had its own crown, with towers that were exquisitely carved with the most intricate designs. As they passed through the gateway, which was made of macaroons and candied fruits, silver soldiers presented arms in their honor, and a little man in a brocade coat threw his arms around the Nutcracker and said, "Welcome, my prince! Welcome to Candytown!"

Marie wondered why the Nutcracker was called a prince by such a distinguished person. Then she heard a loud, joyous clamor from voices all around her and such laughing and singing that she just had to ask young Drosselmeier what it all meant.

"Oh, it's nothing, dear Miss Stahl-baum," he said. "Candytown is a big city, full of merrymaking. This sort of thing goes on every day. Let's continue on a little farther." They stopped by the market-place, where all the houses were round and made of delicately filigreed sugarwork, with bal-conies one above the other, run-ning all the way up to the top. In the center of the market was a square with a mon-umental cake shaped like an obelisk in the middle, surrounded by fountains which bubbled over with lemonade and other beverages. Alongside the market footpaths were streams of cus-tard which could be scooped up with a big spoon. But best of all were the delightful townspeo-ple who shouted and laughed and sang —people who came from every nation and walk of life, ladies and gentlemen alike, Greeks, Armenians, Austrians, Chinese, officers, clergymen, and shepherds, all beautifully dressed and having a wonderful time.

The commotion peaked at one particular corner, as the great mogul passed in a carriage carried by four men, with ninety-three noblemen following in attendance along with seven hundred servants. Unfortunately, five hundred members of the Fishermen's Guild were having a festival on the opposite corner. So when the great mogul decided to direct his entourage across the street, and *another* procession, for the Glories of Nature, began marching toward the obelisk singing, "Hail, all hail the magnificent sun!" with a full orchestra in tow, there were just too many people in one place. Consequently, there was pushing and shoving until cries of pain arose from the crowd; for one of the fishermen had accidentally knocked off a Brahmin's head, and the great mogul had nearly been run down by a pudding man! The throng grew wilder and wilder till the man in brocade climbed atop the obelisk and shouted very loudly three times: "Pastrycook! Pastrycook! Pastrycook!"

Immediately there was quiet. Everybody tried to straighten himself as best he could and disentangle the different parades. The Brahmin's head was stuck back on, and people went on celebrating as before.

"Why did that man yell 'Pastrycook,' Mr. Drosselmeier?" asked Marie.

"Dearest Miss Stahlbaum," said the Nutcracker, "here, 'pastrycook' is what we call the power that rules the destiny of these happy people. The mere mention of the name stops everyone from dwelling on earthly matters, such as blows to the head and small injuries and so on, and causes them to consider the nature of man and the course of his ultimate destiny."

They went on to a castle with a hundred shining towers, and Marie couldn't help uttering a cry of admiration as it came into view. Bouquets of violets, narcissus, tulips, and carnations decorated the outside, their rich colors showing off the rose-tinted white walls splendidly. The center dome as well as each one of the pointed towers was sprinkled with thousands of sparkling gold and silver stars.

"And now," announced the Nutcracker, "last but not least, we come to Marzipan Castle!"

Marie noticed that one of the castle's principal towers was missing a roof. Little men on a scaffold of cinnamon sticks were busy replacing it.

"What happened up there?" she asked.

The Nutcracker explained. "Not long ago," he said, "this castle was

threatened with total destruction. Sweet Tooth, the giant, bit off the top of that tower and was about to start in on the great dome. The people of Candytown had to give him a whole quarter of the town, not to mention a large slice of Sugar Plum Grove, to keep him from finishing it off."

Soft, beautiful music floated out of the castle, and twelve pages appeared with torches made of clove sticks, lighting up the outside. Each one had a lovely pearl for a head, a body made of emeralds and rubies, and feet of pure gold. After them, four ladies about the size of Marie's Miss Clara approached. They were so exquisitely dressed that Marie felt they could be no less than royal princesses. They embraced the Nutcracker, tears of gladness in their eyes, and cried, "Oh, dearest prince! Beloved brother!"

The Nutcracker wiped away tears of his own, then took Marie by the hand and addressed his sisters from the heart: "This is Miss Marie Stahlbaum, the daughter of a very distinguished doctor. She has saved my life. If she hadn't thrown her slipper at exactly the right moment, and if she hadn't found me a sword, I would be cold in my grave right now, bitten to death by the accursed Mouse King. I ask you, can Princess

Pirlipat, princess though she is, compare with Miss Stahlbaum in beauty, goodness, and true virtue? I say emphatically 'No.'"

The ladies cried "No!" in unison and hugged Marie, sobbing and crying out, "Thank you for saving our brother, good Miss Stahlbaum!"

They led Marie and the Nutcracker into the castle, to a hall where the walls were made of sparkling crystal. But what Marie liked best was the furniture. The prettiest little chairs, bureaus, and writing tables, all made of cedar or brazilwood and covered with golden flowers, were placed about the room most elegantly. The princesses made Marie and their brother sit down while they prepared a banquet to welcome them. They brought out cups and dishes of delicate Japanese porcelain, and spoons, knives, forks, graters and stew pots all made of silver and gold. Taking fruits, nuts, and sweets that Marie had never seen before, they squeezed the fruit daintily by hand, grated the spices, and washed the almonds in a way that won Marie's admiration for their skill. She secretly wished that she could assist the princesses in their work and so have helped with these pies herself. Just then, as if reading her mind, one of the Nutcracker's sisters looked up and said, "Good friend, savior of our brother, would you mind pounding some of this sugar candy with us?"

Marie joined them gladly and ground the candy into a sweet paste. The sounds of the work for the banquet blended into a rhythmic song, and the Nutcracker added his voice to it by telling them in great detail about the awful battle he'd fought against the army of the Mouse King. He told of how his troops had let him down, how he had almost been bitten to death, and how Marie had sacrificed several of those dear to her to help him.

Even though Marie was listening carefully, she found it harder and harder to hear the Nutcracker's voice or the sound of her own grinding. They seemed to be getting farther and farther away from her. Then a silvery mist arose in the hall like clouds, and the princesses, the pages, the Nutcracker, and she herself were all floating. There was a buzzing and humming around her that gradually faded away, and she seemed to be ascending up—up—up on waves of silver, rising higher and higher.

Conclusion

With a *poof!* Marie fell down from a great height. It was quite a landing. But when she opened her eyes, she saw she was in her own bed! It was broad daylight, and her mother was standing at her bedside.

"That was quite a sleep you had," she said. "Breakfast has been ready for hours!"

Of course, dear reader, you know what happened. Marie, amazed by all the wonders she had seen, had finally fallen asleep in the Marzipan Castle; and the pages, or maybe the princesses themselves, had carried her home and put her to bed.

"Oh, Mama," said Marie, "what a lot of places young Mr. Drosselmeier has shown me—and what beautiful places they are!" And she told her mother all about where she had been, in much the same way I have told you.

Her mother listened with a look of astonishment and, when Marie had finished, said, "You've had a long, beautiful dream, Marie, but now it's time to forget about it."

Marie insisted that it was not just a dream, so her mother took her by the hand and led her out of bed to the glass cupboard downstairs. She

pointed to the Nutcracker sitting motionless on the shelf and said, "Honestly, Marie. How can you believe that a wooden figure can come to life?"

"But Mama," said Marie, "don't you see? The Nutcracker is young Mr. Drosselmeier from Nuremberg, Godpapa's nephew." Marie's father looked up from his newspaper and laughed right along with Marie's mother.

Marie turned to her father and said, "Go ahead and laugh at poor Nutcracker, Father, but he spoke very highly of *you*. When we were at Marzipan Castle and he introduced me to his sisters, the princesses, he said you were a very distinguished doctor."

This made her father laugh even harder, and soon Louise and Fritz joined in. Marie ran out of the room and came back holding the Mouse King's seven crowns. She handed them to her mother and cried, "Look, Mama! These are the Mouse King's seven crowns! The Nutcracker gave them to me last night as proof of his victory."

Her mother gazed in amazement at the little crowns, which were made of a brilliant, unknown metal and fashioned more intricately than any human hands could possibly manage. Dr. Stahlbaum couldn't stop looking at them either, and they both asked their daughter to tell them exactly where she'd gotten them. Marie could only repeat her story, until her father scolded her for lying to them. Marie started to cry and said, "But I'm *not* lying! It's the truth!"

Just then, the door opened and Godpapa Drosselmeier came in, shouting, "Hello, hello! What's all this? My little Marie crying? What's the matter?"

Dr. Stahlbaum told him about Marie's imaginings and showed him the crowns. As soon as Drosselmeier saw them, he said, "Nonsense!

These are the crowns I used to wear on my watch chain. I gave them to Marie for her second birthday. Don't you remember?"

None of them did. Marie, however, seeing that her mother and father seemed to believe her godpapa, went up to him and said, "You know all about it, Godpapa. Tell them. Tell them that the Nutcracker is your nephew, young Mr. Drosselmeier from Nuremberg, and that he was the one who gave me the crowns."

But her godpapa shook his head angrily and said, "Such nonsense!" Marie's father took her aside and said, "Look here, Marie. I want you to stop this foolishness right now. I won't tolerate another minute of it, and if I ever hear you say that that idiotic Nutcracker is your godfather's nephew, I'll throw it—and all your other toys, including Miss Clara—out the window. Do you understand?"

After that, Marie fell silent and didn't mention it again, though she found it impossible to put out of her mind. I'm sorry to say that even Fritz turned his back on his little sister when she wanted to talk about the things she'd seen and the places that had made her so happy. Rather than listen, he'd say "Stupid goose" under his breath—completely forgetting his usual kindness and patience. Sadly, he no longer believed his sister and held a formal ceremony to take back what he'd said to his soldiers on the Nutcracker's behalf. He gave them back their plumes and reinstated their right to play the official marching call whenever they chose.

Marie dared not speak about her adventures, but they filled her head so that the sweet music of that happy land rang in her ears. Her memories were so vivid that when they came back to haunt her, she sat quietly absorbed within herself. Everyone told her that no good would come of her being such a daydreamer.

One day when Godpapa Drosselmeier was there repairing one of the clocks, Marie was sitting beside the glass cupboard, lost in her dreams. "Oh, dear Mr. Drosselmeier," she said, gazing at the Nutcracker, "if you had given up your handsome looks for *my* sake, I wouldn't despise you the way Princess Pirlipat did! I should love you all the more instead."

"Such nonsense!" cried Godpapa Drosselmeier, but as he spoke, a great tremor shook the earth so that Marie fell from her chair in a faint. When she awoke, her mother was helping her up.

"How could a big girl like you fall off her chair? Come and say hello to Godpapa Drosselmeier's nephew. He just arrived from Nuremberg."

Marie looked up. Her godpapa was wearing his scarlet coat and glass wig and smiling broadly. Next to him was a slight but very handsome young gentleman. He had pale white skin with rosy cheeks and wore a beautiful red coat trimmed with gold lace. His stockings were white silk, and in his lapel was a small bouquet of flowers. Marie wondered at the long pigtail hanging down his back, and at the sword at his side, which seemed to be made of jewels. What caused her even more wonder were the lovely toys he'd brought for her—the very ones that had been eaten by the Mouse King—as well as a beautiful saber for Fritz! He cracked nuts for everyone at dinner, and even the hardest shells were no problem for him. He simply placed the nut in his mouth with his left hand and tugged at his pigtail with his right, and *crack!*—it fell in pieces.

Marie blushed at the sight of this charming gentleman, but she turned an even deeper crimson when he asked her to join him by the glass cupboard after dinner.

"Run along, children," said Godpapa Drosselmeier. "Now that the clocks are fixed, there's no reason you shouldn't go and play."

As soon as young Drosselmeier was alone with Marie, he went down on one knee and said, "My most dearly beloved Miss Stahlbaum! I am the fortunate Drosselmeier whose life you saved on this very spot. When you said that in spite of my ugliness, you would not have despised me the way Princess Pirlipat did, I was transformed from the pathetic Nutcracker

back into my former self. Lovely lady, please marry me and be my queen. Share my kingdom and my heart, and return with me to Marzipan Castle, where I am now king."

Marie took his hand and brought him to his feet, saying, "Dear Mr. Drosselmeier, you are most kind. I am very fond of your country and its charming, funny people, and I accept your hand."

They were formally engaged, and when a year and a day had passed, he came and carried her off in a golden coach drawn by silver horses. Thousands of the most beautiful dolls and figurines danced at the wedding, dressed in pearls and diamonds. To this day, Marie is the queen of Christmas Wood and reigns from Marzipan Castle—the place where she discovered what wonderful and extraordinary things await those who have eyes to see them.

ILLUSTRATOR'S NOTE

I was raised primarily on the magic of two very different illustrators: N. C. Wyeth and Arthur Rackham. One of my earliest and favorite childhood memories is of lying on my parents' bed, listening to my father read *King Arthur*. He would dutifully pause at the prints of Wyeth's paintings and let my sister, brothers and me examine them very carefully. Those pictures would come alive for me and provide passageways for the imagination to wander back in time. Over the years, I learned about and fell in love with the works of many artists, but it was the lasting impact of those first two giants that had the most profound effect on how I work, or would like to work—not so much their technique as their ability to illustrate the text and, simultaneously, tell their own story.

The story of *Nutcracker* deals with two worlds: one real, the other fantastical. As the two are interwoven, some of the imagery is a little wild. My intention was to create illustrations that appropriately represent that dreamlike mingling of both worlds. I found that the real magic of the story could best be brought to life visually through the children's toys. Inventing and designing Old World German toys, especially the kind that Drosselmeier himself might have patiently constructed for Fritz and Marie, was without doubt the most intriguing part of illustrating this book. There is something about those ancient wind-up toys that makes it possible to believe that toy cabinets really do come alive with mysterious activity late at night, after everyone has gone to bed.

Although I did consult some reference books on clothing and architecture, in addition to toys of the period, I was interested in inventing as much as I could, so the images are based only loosely on what I found.

I'm grateful for having had the opportunity to illustrate a classic of this stature. My thanks to all the patient folks who lent support and put up with me for the past seventeen months.

CARTER GOODRICH